How Squirrels got their tails

Story by

Lindsay Todeschini McCormack

Long ago,

deep in the forest on the top of
Hawks Hill there was a
circle of trees.
There was a tree in which
Lindsay, the short-tailed

LITTLE EARED
GRAY SQUIRREL

lived.

It Was a COLD winter Morning

when Lindsay was making a **Steaming** pot of refreshing hot tea. Lindsay was just about to sit down when all **Of** a sudden

she heard Footsteps

coming towards her tree.

Calmly she walked over to her window and saw Craig, the Beaver with a **chainsaw**. Lindsay **did not** expect him. "He ran out of firewood— and is coming right for **my beautiful house!**" said Lindsay.

Lindsay shuddered with **FRIGHT**. She was rapidly packing her things when she **heard** the chainsaw turn on. Before she knew it, her house was on the **ground**.

Lindsay was crying because her beautiful house was **ruined**. Craig saw the tree was **hollow** and did not take it. He did not realize it was Lindsay's house. Lindsay tried to get up from under the tree, but **she was stuck**. She cried **louder**.

Lauren, the fox heard LINDSAY CRY.

She ran over to Lindsay's house. Lauren saw Lindsay and her house on the SnoWy ground. Lindsay said, "Craig, the Beaver chopped doWn my house and it fell on my tail". Lauren tried to get Lindsay's tail out from under the tree

Lindsay's best friend,
DANIELLE the groundhog
came over to help. Danielle kept
digging and digging while Lauren
pulled and pulled on Lindsay's arms.
Danielle and Lauren were SO tired but

they did not give up.

While all of this COMMOTION was going on, two trolls were watching from the clouds. They knew they could help. They asked the QUEEN TROLL if they could go help Lindsay and her friends.

Queen Troll said, "GO, but don't let anybody SEE YOU". The trolls looked down from the clouds. They saw Lindsay crying, Lauren pulling and Danielle digging. The two trolls sprinkled magical dust on the tree and Lindsay's tail slipped out.

Her tail was STRETCHED SO LONG from all that pulling.

The trolls started LAUGHING because Lindsay's tail was so long. Lauren and Danielle told Lindsay her tail looked different but she was still a beautiful squirrel. Lindsay thanked her friends for being so kind and helping her through a tough time.

The Trolls realized the change to Lindsay's tail had a special meaning of friendship and kindness. The animal friends stuck together, did not give up and worked together. So they decided to grant all the squirrels in the land long fluffy tails.

That is the magical story on how squirrels got their tails.

By:
Lindsay
Todeschini
5th grade 1993

About the Author

Lindsay Todeschini McCormack originally wrote *How Squirrels Got Their Tails* as an English project when she was ten years old in the 5th grade. She went on to graduate from LeMoyne College and now lives with her husband, Patrick, her twins, Eva Marie and Leo Patrick, and their dog, Nelli.

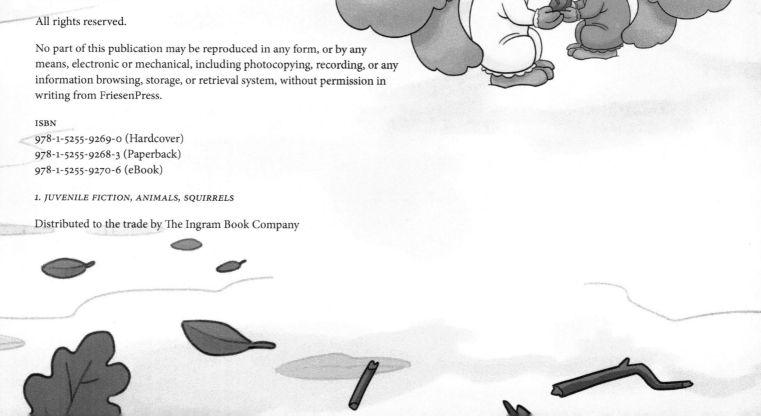

FriesenPress

Suite 300 - 990 Fort St
Victoria, BC, V8V 3K2
Canada

www.friesenpress.com

ISBN
978-1-5255-9269-0 (Hardcover)
978-1-5255-9268-3 (Paperback)
978-1-5255-9270-6 (eBook)

1. JUVENILE FICTION, ANIMALS, SQUIRRELS

Distributed to the trade by The Ingram Book Company

CPSIA information can be obtained
at www.ICGtesting.com
Printed in the USA
BVHW020247070521
606649BV00009B/1640